This book
belongs to

Walt Disney's Sleeping Beauty

Adapted by Lisa Ann Marsoli

MOUSE WORKS

Once upon a time, there lived a kind king and gentle queen who longed to have a child. After many years of waiting, their wish was granted, and a daughter was born. They named her Aurora, which means "dawn," because she brightened their lives with happiness just as the sun brightens the day.

A great holiday was proclaimed to celebrate the princess's birth, and visitors were welcomed from all over the kingdom. Among those journeying to the palace were the three good fairies Merryweather, Fauna, and Flora.

King Hubert, who ruled the neighboring kingdom, and his young son, Prince Phillip, were also invited to attend.

People streamed into the palace,
bringing gifts and good wishes to
Princess Aurora and her parents.
Royal and common folk alike wanted
to share the joy of King Stefan and
his queen, and to see the long-awaited
princess.

When King Hubert and Prince Phillip arrived, King Stefan welcomed his old friend warmly. Both kings realized that their longtime dream of uniting their two kingdoms could now come true. Then and there, they declared that Princess Aurora and Prince Phillip were betrothed.

Soon the trumpets sounded, and
three sparkling balls of light floated
into the room. Out of them emerged
Flora, Fauna, and Merryweather,
ready to bestow their special gifts
on the infant princess.

Flora approached the cradle first. "Little princess," she said softly, "my gift shall be the gift of beauty . . . gold of sunshine in your hair, and lips that shame the red rose." Then Flora waved her wand, and flowers showered down upon the sleeping beauty.

Now it was Fauna's turn. "My gift shall be the gift of song," she said. And as Fauna waved her wand above the cradle, a flock of colorful birds magically appeared.

At last it was Merryweather's
turn to present a gift to the baby.
The short, plump fairy marched
up to the cradle and began,
"Sweet princess, my gift shall be . . ."

But before Merryweather could
continue, a great gust of wind blew
open the doors and swept into the
room. There was a flash of lightning,
a crack of thunder, and then darkness.
Suddenly, a bright flame burned in
the middle of the great hall.

The flame took the shape of a woman dressed in a long, black cape and carrying a staff. The feeling of evil that surrounded her filled the onlookers with dread.

"It's Maleficent!" gasped Fauna.

"I was quite hurt at not being invited to your party," the wicked fairy began, addressing the king. "But to show I bear no ill will, I, too, shall bestow a gift on the child."

"Listen well, all of you," she commanded, her voice echoing throughout the hall. "The princess shall indeed grow in grace and beauty, beloved by those who know her. But before the sun sets on her sixteenth birthday, she shall prick her finger on the spindle of a spinning wheel . . . and die."

"No!" cried the queen, running to the cradle and scooping her baby into her arms. But Maleficent looked on, unmoved by the queen's anguish, and laughed a cruel and heartless laugh.

King Stefan could bear it no longer. "Seize that creature!" he shouted.

Before the guards could reach her,
Maleficent disappeared in a burst
of fire and smoke. Her pet raven
circled over the spot where she had
stood, then flew away.

The queen held the princess in
her arms. She could scarcely believe
that she might ever lose the daughter
for whom she had waited so long.

Flora broke the stunned silence. "Don't despair, Your Majesties. Merryweather still has her gift to give the princess." Merryweather's powers were not strong enough to undo Maleficent's evil curse, but the fairies knew she could soften it a little.

"Sweet princess," Merryweather said softly, "a ray of hope there still may be in this the gift I give to thee. Not in death, but just in sleep, the fateful prophecy you will keep, and from this slumber you shall wake, when true love's kiss the spell shall break."

Even with Merryweather's help,
King Stefan remained fearful for
his daughter's life. To prevent the
evil curse from coming true, he
ordered that every spinning wheel
in the kingdom be burned. That
night, thousands of spinning wheels
were collected and brought to the
palace. As King Stefan and the
queen watched the bonfire, they
felt certain their daughter would
now be safe.

But the good fairies feared that burning the spinning wheels alone would not keep Princess Aurora safe from Maleficent's curse. They knew they had to devise some sort of plan to save the princess. Flora came up with a solution.

Flora told the other fairies what they must do. "We'll disguise ourselves as peasant women and pretend Princess Aurora is an orphan we have adopted. We'll live deep in the forest — Maleficent will never expect to find her there!"

"Then, on the princess's sixteenth birthday, when the curse ends, we will return her to the palace. Of course, the king and queen will object," she said gently, "but when we explain that it's the only way . . ."

Flora demonstrated her plan by turning the other fairies into peasant women.

It was not easy to convince the king and queen of the plan to let the fairies take the princess. Sixteen years would be a long time to be without their child. Knowing that they had to do everything they could to protect their daughter, they finally agreed.

One evening soon after, Flora, Fauna, and Merryweather carried the baby princess away into the night. With heavy hearts, King Stefan and his queen watched as the figures of the fairies grew small in the distance and disappeared into the forest.

And so, for sixteen years, the whereabouts of Princess Aurora remained a secret. In the heart of the forest, in a woodcutter's cottage, the good fairies carried out their well-laid plan. There they raised the princess as their own, calling her by the name Briar Rose. They never revealed to her anything about the king and queen, her royal heritage, or Maleficent's curse.

What's more, the three good fairies kept their true identities a secret from Briar Rose, and stopped using their magic altogether. They bathed her in a wooden tub, and they cleaned and scrubbed and did everything the way ordinary people do so that Briar Rose would never suspect that they were different from everyone else.

Briar Rose grew, and became everything the fairies had bestowed upon her when she was a baby. She was not only beautiful, but kind, and wherever she went, she carried a song in her heart.

Briar Rose's sixteenth birthday was drawing near, and the good fairies knew that soon they would need to return the princess to the palace. There, she would resume her rightful identity and marry Prince Phillip, as had been arranged by her father so many years before.

"It seems like only yesterday that we brought her here," sighed Merryweather.

The fairies would be sad to see their time with Briar Rose end. She had filled their lives with so much joy and laughter—things that the evil Maleficent would never understand.

High on the Forbidden Mountain, Maleficent had never stopped searching for Princess Aurora. Year after year, her henchmen had scoured the kingdom for the girl without success.

"We've searched mountains, forests, and houses," the leader told Maleficent, "and all the cradles, too."

"Fools! Idiots! Imbeciles!"
Maleficent screamed, suddenly
realizing that for sixteen years
they had been searching for a baby!

Maleficent's raven swooped down
and perched on the arm of her throne.

"Oh, my pet," the wicked fairy began,
"you are my last hope. Circle far and
wide. Search for a maid of sixteen
with hair as gold as sunshine and
lips as red as a rose. Go, and do not
fail me."

As Maleficent watched the raven
fly out through the open window,
she believed her pet would find the
missing princess at last.

At the cottage in the forest, Flora, Fauna, and Merryweather were busy making plans for Briar Rose's sixteenth birthday party. They wanted to surprise her, so they sent her out into the forest to pick wild berries while they got everything ready.

Fauna was going to make the birthday cake, and Flora was going to sew a special birthday dress for Briar Rose to wear. Once Merryweather understood that she was to be the model, she demanded that they use their magic so that everything would be perfect.

"No magic," Flora insisted. She knew that until the princess was back safely at the castle, the fairies still needed to keep their identities a secret.

While the three fairies were busy at the cottage, Briar Rose wandered through the forest, picking wild berries. Some animal friends kept her company, and when her basket was full, she sang them a song. She sang a lovely melody about the man of her dreams.

Nearby, a young prince heard Briar Rose's sweet voice drifting through the trees. "Who is that singing, Samson?" the prince asked his horse. "Let's go find out."

It took some coaxing, but soon Samson broke into a gallop, carrying the prince closer and closer to the sound of the enchanting voice.

Briar Rose continued singing her song, daydreaming and dancing with the imaginary man she would one day love. She did not hear the prince come up behind her. When he joined in her singing, she was quite startled!

"I'm sorry," the prince said. "I didn't mean to frighten you."

The prince and Briar Rose danced and sang together. Then, hand in hand, they strolled through the forest, with Briar Rose's animal friends following close behind. It was easy to see that the two were falling in love.

When the prince asked Briar Rose her name, she realized she didn't know his name, or anything else about him. She suddenly remembered that the fairies had warned her never to speak to strangers. So Briar Rose turned and began to run away.

"But when will I see you again?" the prince called after her.

Briar Rose stopped and thought a moment. "This evening at the cottage in the glen," she told him. Then she disappeared into the forest.

Back at the cottage, Flora, Fauna, and Merryweather were in a panic. Fauna looked at the dress Flora had just made and said, as politely as she could, "That's not exactly the way it is in the book."

Fauna's cake was in no better shape. It leaned so badly to one side that she had to brace it with a broom. Even so, the icing and candles slid off the top of the cake and down the broom handle.

"I've had enough of this nonsense!" declared Merryweather, peeking out from the top of the ridiculous dress. "I'm going to get our magic wands!" And with that, she rushed up to the attic.

When Merryweather returned, the fairies shut all the doors and windows and drew the curtains. Then, certain that no one could see them, they set about making everything perfect — with a little help from their magic wands.

Flora directed the ribbon and scissors until she had created a beautiful dress for Briar Rose.

Fauna waved her magic wand over the table. "Eggs, flour, milk. Just do what it says," she said to the ingredients, pointing her wand at the cookbook.

In no time at all, a magnificent birthday cake appeared.

But there was one slight problem. Merryweather decided that Briar Rose's dress should be blue, not pink. She waved her magic wand, and instantly the dress changed color.

But then Flora decided that she liked the dress the way she had originally made it — pink. With a wave of her wand, she changed the dress back.

"Make it blue!" Merryweather commanded her magic wand, and the dress changed color again.

Back and forth the colors went. Sparkles from the wands flew around
the room and up the chimney. The chimney! It was the one place the
fairies had forgotten to seal off.

Just then, Maleficent's raven flew overhead and saw the colorful
sparkles coming from the cottage. Looking more closely, he knew that
they were made by the magic of the three good fairies — and that he had
found the princess at last. He raced back to tell his mistress, the evil Maleficent.

Soon after, Briar Rose returned home from the forest.

"Surprise! Surprise!" the good fairies shouted when Briar Rose walked through the door.

"Oh, you darlings!" Briar Rose exclaimed when she saw the cake and the dress. "Everything is so wonderful! Just wait until you meet him. He's coming here tonight!" she announced dreamily.

Then Briar Rose told the fairies all about the young man she had met in the forest.

"She's in love," the fairies said sadly. They knew it was time to tell Briar Rose the truth.

At last, when they were finished, she knew that she was really Princess Aurora, and that she was already betrothed to Prince Phillip.

"Tonight we must take you back to your father and mother," Flora told her softly.

Briar Rose wept, for she knew she would never see her young man again.

At dusk, the three fairies and Princess Aurora set out on the journey to the palace. As the princess walked, she thought only of the young man she had met that day.

Back at the palace, King Stefan and King Hubert were toasting the upcoming marriage of their children. But King Hubert's merriment came to an end when Prince Phillip arrived and, taking his father aside, announced that he was in love with a girl he had just met in the forest.

Later that night, Princess Aurora and the fairies arrived at the palace and managed to slip inside. Then the fairies left the princess in a room where they thought she would be safe. But no sooner had the fairies left than a wisp of light appeared in the room. In a trance, Princess Aurora followed the light through a secret panel and up a winding staircase to a hidden room. There stood the cruel Maleficent—next to a spinning wheel!

"Touch the spindle! Touch it, I say!" Maleficent commanded. The princess obeyed, and pricked her finger on the spindle's sharp point.

The three fairies returned to the room where they had left the princess, but she was nowhere to be found. They quickly followed the path that she had taken to the hidden tower, and were met by a gleeful Maleficent.

"Here's your precious princess!" she proclaimed as she stepped aside to reveal the princess lying on the floor. Content to see the shock on the faces of the three fairies, Maleficent disappeared in flames and smoke.

Tears rolled down the cheeks of the three good fairies.

"Poor King Stefan, and the poor queen," sobbed Fauna.

"They'll be heartbroken when they find out," added Merryweather.

"They're not going to," replied Flora. "We'll put them all to sleep until the princess is awakened."

The fairies made themselves very small, and flew about the palace.
They waved their magic wands over the guards, the royal subjects,
even the king and queen, putting them all into a deep sleep.

Just before King Hubert was about to go to sleep, Flora overheard
him trying to tell King Stefan about the peasant girl Prince Phillip
insisted he was going to marry.

Suddenly, Flora realized that Princess Aurora's young man from the forest was really Prince Phillip. Then she remembered that the princess had said he would be returning to the cottage that very night.

"Fauna! Merryweather!" she called. "Come with me. We've got to get back to the cottage!" The fairies flew as fast as they could, hoping to find Prince Phillip and tell him the truth.

But Prince Phillip was already at the door of the cottage in the glen.
When he knocked, a voice from inside called for him to come in.
With love in his heart, the prince opened the door and went inside.

Before he realized what was happening, the prince was surrounded by Maleficent's horrible henchmen. They tied him with heavy rope and gagged him with a cloth.

Maleficent stepped out of the darkness and approached the captured prince. She knew that he alone had the power to break the spell she had placed on Princess Aurora. All he had to do was to place true love's kiss on the princess's lips, and she would awake. Maleficent had to stop him!

"Away with him!" she commanded her henchmen, cackling. "But gently, my pets. I have plans for our royal guest."

Moments later, the three good fairies reached the cottage, finding only the prince's hat inside. "Maleficent!" cried Flora. "She must have taken Prince Phillip to Forbidden Mountain!" The fairies knew it would be dangerous to go there, but they also knew they had no other choice. They had to rescue the prince.

By now Prince Phillip was chained to a dungeon wall at Maleficent's castle on Forbidden Mountain.

"Oh, come, now. Why so melancholy?" Maleficent taunted him. And to make him despair even more, she told him of Princess Aurora, asleep in King Stefan's palace. "See the gracious whim of fate," she continued. "Why, she is the same peasant girl who only yesterday won your heart."

The prince strained against his shackles, knowing he had to escape somehow and save the princess.

Maleficent took great joy in seeing the prince's helplessness. "I'll just leave you with your happy thoughts," she told him as she left the dungeon.

At that moment, Flora, Fauna, and Merryweather flew down from a crack in the dungeon wall where they had been hiding. "Shh! No time to explain!" they told the startled prince.

Flora used her wand to break the shackles on his wrists, while Fauna released his ankles.

"The road to your true love holds still more dangers, which you must face alone," Flora said. Then she waved her wand, and a sword and shield magically appeared in Prince Phillip's hands. "So arm yourself with this enchanted Shield of Virtue and this mighty Sword of Truth. These weapons will help you triumph over evil."

Armed with the sword and shield, the prince set off to save the princess, but first he had to escape Maleficent's dangerous domain. With the fairies' help, he dodged arrows, lightning bolts, and falling rocks. But no matter what the angry Maleficent put in his way, the prince continued on. He was determined to rescue Princess Aurora.

When Prince Phillip neared the palace of King Stefan, Maleficent placed a wall of thorns in his path. But the prince cut the branches with his Sword of Truth, and was able to pass through unharmed.

Maleficent watched as the prince sped toward the palace bridge, but she would let him go no farther. With a blinding explosion of flames, she turned herself into a fierce, fire-breathing dragon. It was the most hideous beast the prince had ever seen.

"Now you shall deal with me!" the dragon roared.

Phillip raised his Shield of Virtue and charged at the dragon. In reply, the creature opened its enormous mouth and hissed great blasts of fire at the prince. He fell, but quickly returned to his feet and dodged the dragon's enormous snapping jaws.

The prince tried to turn and retreat, but he found himself cornered on the edge of a cliff. The fairies watched anxiously, terrified for his life.

All at once, an explosion of fire from the enraged dragon's mouth swept the prince's shield into the abyss below. The beast gathered its breath, preparing to finish off the prince with one last blast of flame.

The prince took aim with his Sword of Truth and hurled it at the dragon. The blade pierced the dragon's heart, and the beast fell back in agony, plunging over the edge of the cliff.

Now Prince Phillip could fulfill his quest. He hurried through the palace gates past the sleeping guards and servants and royal subjects. Then, led by the three fairies, he climbed the winding staircase to the tower chamber where Princess Aurora lay sleeping. Prince Phillip knelt by the bed and kissed her gently on the lips.

Princess Aurora opened her eyes and smiled at her prince. Instantly, the fairies began waking up everyone in the kingdom.

"Now, you were saying, Hubert . . ." yawned King Stefan.

"Ah, yes," King Hubert continued. "My son Phillip says he's going to marry—"

But before King Hubert could explain that his son was intending to marry a peasant girl, the trumpets sounded. All eyes turned to the grand staircase, where Princess Aurora and Prince Phillip made their entrance, arm in arm.

"It's Aurora! She's here!" cried King Stefan.

The princess and her parents rushed into each other's arms, joyfully reunited at last.

King Hubert tried to ask Prince Phillip about the peasant girl he wanted to marry. "What does this mean, boy?" he asked. But before his son could answer, Princess Aurora went to the king and gave him a big kiss on the cheek. King Hubert blushed with pleasure, and forgot whatever it was he had been saying.

When it was announced that the prince and princess wished to marry, the two kings were overjoyed. Their kingdoms would be united once and for all.

Prince Phillip and Princess Aurora danced together as both kings, the queen, and all their loyal subjects looked on. Flora, Fauna, and Merryweather watched the festivities from a balcony high above.

"I just love happy endings," Fauna said with a sigh. And they all agreed that this certainly was the happiest ending that anyone could remember.

Published by Mouse Works, an imprint of Penguin Books USA Inc., 375 Hudson Street, New York, New York 10014
Mouse Works™ is a trademark of The Walt Disney Company.
Printed in the United States of America.

ISBN 0-453-03168-4

10 9 8 7 6 5 4 3 2